WILLIAM HUSSEY

THE NIGHTMARE EATER

EDGE
FRANKLIN WATTS

LONDON · SYDNEY

First published in 2013
by Franklin Watts

Text © William Hussey 2013
Cover design by Peter Scoulding

Franklin Watts
338 Euston Road
London NW1 3BH

Franklin Watts Australia
Level 17/207 Kent Street
Sydney, NSW 2000

A CIP catalogue record for this book
is available from the British Library.

A-Digit/istockphoto: front cover b & back cover t.
jpa1999/istockphoto: front cover c.

ISBN: 978 1 4451 2311 0
eBook ISBN: 978 1 4451 2314 1
Library eBook ISBN: 978 1 4451 2576 3

1 3 5 7 9 10 8 6 4 2

Printed in Great Britain

Franklin Watts is a division of
Hachette Children's Books,
an Hachette UK company.
www.hachette.co.uk

THE NIGHTMARE EATER

FROM THE AUTHOR OF WITCHFINDER

EDGE / RIVETS

Also by William Hussey:

Witchfinder: Dawn of the Demontide

Witchfinder: Gallows at Twilight

Witchfinder: The Last Nightfall

Haunted

For Joe Gartshore: ravenous reader and righteous dude

CONTENTS

CHAPTER ONE

The fairground buzzed around
Tomasz Kaczmarek like a gigantic
glow-in-the-dark bug. Laughter
bubbled out of the hall of mirrors,
screams crashed down from the
roller coaster, and candyfloss
sugared the night air. Tomasz

squeezed through wide-eyed crowds until at last he glimpsed the horror house. There, at the very edge of the fair, he thought back to a promise he had made long ago...

"I've told you many tales, my boy." Aleksander Kaczmarek reached down and gathered his grandson onto his knee. "Legends like that of the witch Baba Jaga, who takes children to her chicken-leg house and eats them by the light of the moon! But you know, Tomasz, these stories are not just to entertain. They have a purpose..." The old man nodded sadly. "Now, you have asked if I will take you to this fairground—"

"Yes!" Tomasz bounced excitedly. "I saw a poster at the bus stop. It said they had a helter-skelter and something called a 'waltzer' and a—"

"You read all this yourself?" Aleksander laughed. "Your English is better than mine."

"Course it is! I was born here."

"Just so. Still, it is clever for a six-year-old to read such words. Your mother is clever, too. And your father, ah, he was the brightest of students..."

Those kind eyes crinkled with pain. A professor of engineering, Tomasz's father had died of cancer when Tomasz was less than a year old. Two weeks later, Aleksander had arrived from Poland to help take care of his precious grandson.

"Where was I?" The old man blinked. "Ah yes, those stories of mine. I tell them to keep you safe, my little Tomasz. To help you recognise evil in all its forms. Today, as I walked past the big park where this man Grimaldi is setting up his fairground, I sensed *it*." Aleksander's hairy nostrils flared, as if he could still detect an ugly stench upon the air. "Somewhere among those rides and stalls, the shadow of evil lurks. So you must swear to me that you will never go near that place. Never!"

Frightened by his grandpa's intensity, Tomasz had given his promise freely...

Now the twelve-year-old Tomasz Kaczmarek turned away from the horror house and glanced at the hill that overlooked the fairground. Up there among the restful dead, the white cross that marked his grandpa's grave would be shining like a beacon in the moonlight.

A beacon warning of danger ahead.

CHAPTER TWO

Tomasz was searching through
his pocket for money to buy
his horror house ticket when
something hard and sticky
crunched against the back of his
head. Turning, he found a half-
eaten toffee apple at his feet, its

red skin broken like the crust of a volcano.

"Bull's eye!" cried Douglas 'Dugs' Duggan. Doubled over in a fit of giggles, the bully pointed a chubby forefinger at his victim. "Smack in the melon!"

Tomasz groaned. "What're *you* doing here?"

His amusement forgotten, Dugs came striding over to where Tomasz stood alone.

Dugs lifted him an inch from the ground. Up close, Tomasz could see bright-headed pimples glowing like LEDs and smell the BO coming from his enemy's armpits.

"I came to check that Tommy Tinkle wouldn't chicken out," Dugs grinned. "You said you'd prove your guts tonight, and if you don't, everyone at school's gonna hear about it."

'Tommy Tinkle': how often had he heard *that* in the past few weeks?

It had all started when, unknown to Tomasz, his mum had come into school to speak with his head of year. Both parent and teacher thought they were alone, but serving detention in the classroom next door, Dugs had overheard everything.

"Doesn't look like you've wet yourself yet," Dugs laughed. "What did your mum call it? 'Night terrors'? Ever since your grandpa passed away last year you've been peeing the bed! Man, that's *so* weak!"

Taking Tomasz by the scruff of the neck, Dugs turned him to face the horror house.

"Every year Grimaldi's comes to town and every year the stories go round." His voice dropped to a whisper. "They say it's the scariest horror house in the world."

During the few minutes in which he'd been loitering at the edges of the fair, Tomasz had seen many curious glances thrown at 'Grimaldi's House of Horrors.'

The exterior had been painted to resemble a cartoonish castle with fake spider webs fluttering above its portcullis entrance. Behind arrow-slit windows, the faces of cheesy mannequin monsters leered down at the crowds. All pretty lame, Tomasz thought. And yet the thrill-seekers gave the phony castle a wide berth, as if they sensed that something darker lurked within its cheap walls.

Dugs shoved him towards the castle.

"I'll wait for you here, Tommy Tinkle."

Tomasz checked his watch: 8:30pm. He had plenty of time before his mum picked him up at nine. He'd told her that he was meeting some mates at the fair; a lie that had won him a smile. Since his grandpa's death, Tomasz had been too distracted by 'night terrors' to give his friends much thought. As soon as he fell asleep, the characters from his grandpa's stories would stir in the mists of his dreams and sap what little courage he had left.

Tomasz stepped up to the ticket booth and slid coins through a hole in the plastic screen.

"One, ple—" Fear trapped the word in his throat.

A string of multicoloured bulbs flashed their garish light against the face of the man in the booth. Crisscrossed with scars, the guy's head looked like it had been stitched together from a hundred different scraps of skin. A big hand reached forward and took Tomasz's money.

"Balfus Grimaldi," the showman grunted. "Welcome to my 'House of Horrors'. Make sure you follow the arrows on the walls and..." He grinned, showing a mouthful of golden teeth. "Have fun!"

Clutching his ticket, Tomasz mounted the steps that led to the castle door. The closer he came, the more pathetic those flimsy webs and moth-eaten mannequins appeared. Nevertheless, he couldn't shake the sense of evil that radiated out from the dark doorway. Was this the same malevolence his grandpa had felt?

At the top of the steps, Tomasz looked back. No sign of Balfus in his ticket booth. If only the same could be said for Dugs. Encircled with chunky rings, the bully's beefy fingers waved Tomasz on. Beyond Dugs, the fairground barked and blared and a thousand lights pushed their bright thumbs into the inkpad of the sky.

Gathering the shreds of his courage, Tomasz stepped into the house of horrors.

CHAPTER THREE

The walls were black, the arrows
luminous green. Tomasz followed
them into a maze of shadows,
a few flickering strip lights the
only source of illumination.
His footsteps clunked down
the narrow corridors while the

grumble of a generator shivered the plywood walls. Was *this* it? At the very least he'd expected a plastic skeleton to drop through the roof! Tomasz felt a crowd of giggles rising in his stomach.

Then, stepping through a doorway, a metal wall descended and his giggles vanished. Tomasz found himself trapped in a windowless chamber about the size of a basketball court. Overhead, a single bulb struggled against the dusty darkness. He was still recovering from the wall's deafening *clang* when Balfus's voice echoed around the room.

"Please remain calm. This is all part of the horror house experience. Please remain calm. This is..." The message continued on a recorded loop.

Weirdest. Fairground. Attraction. Ever! The falling wall had shocked him all right, but this empty room hardly qualified as the scariest horror house in the world...

Something shifted: a figure rising out of the gloom on the far side of the chamber. While Balfus's message bounced from wall to wall, the small, stooped shape gathered substance, like a nightmare willing itself into reality. It started tottering towards him and Tomasz backed up against the metal wall.

Bowling ahead of the figure came an aroma of rotting vegetation, mixed in with the metallic tang of old blood. The kind of scent he had always associated with the witch Baba Jaga from his grandpa's stories.

"Are you there?" asked a reedy voice. "The moon is full and I want you to come to my chicken-leg house..."

Feature by feature, she emerged from the shadows: first, the crook nose with its festering sores; then a nest of bone-white hair laced with autumn leaves; twisted hands like eagles' talons; eyes the colour of burning embers; and finally, thin black lips smeared with the blood of a thousand children.

"Come now, it's almost suppertime."

Before the crone could catch him, the light overhead fizzled and died. Beneath his feet, Tomasz felt the generator splutter until the floorboards ceased to tremble and the recorded message droned to a halt. Terrified, he plunged his hand into his pocket and brought out his mobile phone. That witch was no mannequin, no feeble fright house horror. Either he was going mad or somehow the evil of this place had conjured one of his nightmares into existence.

Tomasz swiped his thumb across the phone and used its screen light as a torch.

The chamber was empty.

"H-hello?" The youthful voice of a stranger broke the stillness. "Is anyone there?"

Was this another phantom plucked

from Tomasz's mind? He didn't think so. For starters, he'd never heard that voice before, either in dreams or reality.

"Who are you?" Tomasz called out.

"My name's Peter Grimaldi. They keep me prisoner here, locked away in the dark. Please, you have to help me. Balfus will get the generator started any minute and the wall will be sealed again. *Hurry!*"

So Grandpa Kaczmarek's nose for evil had served him well: this fairground was indeed hiding a dark secret.

Tomasz rushed across the chamber. To his surprise he found that the back wall was not made of wood but of a reinforced glass, the surface darkly tinted. Like the metal wall which had trapped him, this partition could be raised and lowered, and was presently hovering half a metre off the floor. Tomasz dropped to the ground and rolled under.

"Oh thank you!" came the prisoner's delighted squeal. "Quickly now, the chain!"

Regaining his feet, Tomasz flashed his phone light over a small wooden cell containing a cot bed, a shelf stacked with books and a large comfortable armchair. In the leathery depths of this chair sat a boy dressed in what appeared to be a monk's robe, his features hidden beneath a hood. The prisoner lifted his painfully thin wrist.

"My God!" Tomasz whispered. "Why have they done this to you?"

"Because they're insane."

For now, this explanation was enough. Tomasz examined the manacle binding the prisoner's wrist to a chain attached to the wall. The wood was badly rotted and, if the boy had been stronger, he might easily have freed himself. As it was, it took only a strain and a grunt for Tomasz to wrench the chain from its fitting.

"There! Now we better get moving."

"Of course."

Something in those simple words caused a shiver to ripple along Tomasz's spine. The end of the chain still in his fist, he turned to find the prisoner rising from his chair. Those twig-like fingers grasped the edges of the hood, ready to draw it back.

"But first, I must eat."

CHAPTER FOUR

Almost entirely pupil, the eyes
of Peter Grimaldi sat like dark
saucers in his thin, reptilian face.
They reminded Tomasz of the
huge, soulless eyes of a deep
sea fish, and he guessed that,
in this endless gloom, Peter's

sight might have evolved in just such a way. The scale-skinned creature stepped forward and, with a sickening *crack*, his long mouth dropped open. There was no tongue, no teeth, no tonsils — just a black, dripping hole.

"Such fear." The words slipped like syrup from Peter's lips. "Delicious fear!"

Rooted to the spot, Tomasz felt something inside him lurch forward. His own mouth dropped open and a kind of misty haze siphoned out of his throat and passed into the jaws of the creature. He felt the texture of his nightmares leaving him (Baba Jaga, the were-beasts of Transylvania: all his grandpa's stories), but instead of feeling relieved, he found himself desperate to hold onto them.

Peter's lidless eyes widened as he gorged himself on terror.

Eyes...

Tomasz felt the phone still

clenched in his left hand. With
a huge effort, he thumbed the
screen and pushed the light into
those night-dark orbs.

"Kkkarrrggghhhhh!" the creature
shrieked, and dashed the phone
from Tomasz's grasp. It hit the
ground with a smart crack and the
light died.

In the next instant, the chain
whipped through his fingers and
Tomasz heard the great glass
wall shatter.

CHAPTER FIVE

By the time Tomasz overcame
the shock of what he had just
witnessed, Peter was long gone.
It took several minutes stumbling
around in the dark for Tomasz
to find the way out, where he
was greeted by wave after wave
of screams. There was no sign

of Peter, though the evidence
of his carnage was all around.
At first Tomasz didn't recognise
Douglas Duggan; the bully's body
was so shrivelled it looked like a
thousand-year-old mummy, but
then he saw the chunky rings
clinging to those bony fingers.

A hand grabbed Tomasz's collar
and dragged him behind the
ticket booth. Fresh scars had
been added to the face of Balfus
Grimaldi and the big man was
bleeding freely from a wound at
his throat.

"You let him out!" the showman seethed. "You fool!"

Balfus collapsed into a sitting position and Tomasz knelt beside him.

"Who — *what* is he?"

"My brother."

"Brother?!"

"*Older* brother," Balfus nodded grimly. "Same mother, different fathers. His was an incubus. A dream demon. There isn't really a word for what Peter is. He's like a psychic leech, feeding off the fear of others. I built the horror house to contain him. Behind the glass his powers were weak and he could feed without killing. Though he's immortal, he must eat to survive."

"He makes nightmares real," Tomasz nodded, "then feeds on the terror. But he's a monster! Why would you keep him alive like this?"

"Because he's my brother," Balfus said simply. "And until tonight my plan was foolproof. But then the generator gave out and the glass wall mechanism short-circuited. He has to be stopped."

The showman rolled onto his side and, from some hidden pocket, took out a beautiful shining necklace.

"This is a Morphean amulet. Place it around his neck and my brother will sleep."

Tomasz flinched back from the task. "I can't."

"You must. If Peter gets into the city he'll drain thousands. You released him, boy. Those deaths will be on your head."

Reluctantly, Tomasz accepted the necklace. The delicate chain was silver, the pendant inscribed with strange talismanic symbols. Though his soul shrank against it, he knew that Balfus was right. This slaughter was on his conscience and he had to stop it.

Leaving the injured showman at the booth, he strode out into the fairground of death.

Wild-eyed crowds surged against him. Many caught at his coat, repeating stories of a strange maniacal boy rampaging through the fair. Some said that they had witnessed this monster cutting through whole families with its razor-sharp fingers, while others claimed it used a pitch-black mouth to suck the life from its victims.

Tomasz pushed on.

The wind raced with him between
deserted stalls and rides. Under
every canvas he saw fresh horrors:
husk-like bodies littering the floor
of a shooting gallery; frozen-
faced corpses bunched together
in the still-spinning gondolas of
the waltzer. He paused beside a
merry-go-round where wooden
horses and their dead-eyed riders
revolved in a silent circle. But for
the carousel's hum, everything
seemed still.

Maybe Peter had already left the fair.

He was about to hurry back to Balfus when a fresh scream split the night. His gaze swung to the huge Ferris wheel and the swaying carriage at its summit. Sixty metres from the ground, two figures appeared to be grappling with each other, their distant forms framed by the moon. One was dressed in a monkish robe, the other...

Tomasz renewed his grip on the amulet.

"Mum...?"

CHAPTER SIX

With the amulet in his pocket, Tomasz scrambled up the ladder that ran along the Ferris wheel's supporting tower. On either side empty carriages swung freely, the creak of their hinges like a mournful song. By the time he reached the centre of the wheel, the wind was driving sweat into his eyes. At this midpoint the ladder stopped and he saw that, to reach the topmost carriage, he'd have to climb a huge metallic spoke unaided.

"Better hurry," came Peter's mocking voice. "I'm feeling hungry again!"

Tomasz leapt onto the spoke. Despite its smooth appearance, there were footholds to be found in the rusted iron. Lungs striving, muscles burning, he hauled himself towards the stars. With the last of his strength, he pulled himself into the final carriage and took the amulet from his pocket. Somewhere far below, the last generator failed and the fairground stuttered into darkness.

Struck dumb with terror, Tomasz's mother looked from her son to the creature which held her at the open carriage door. Her heels teetered on the brink as Peter inched her towards the drop.

"I saw her in your mind," he purred. "And I found her waiting at the gate. Do you understand your greatest fear, Tomasz?"

He pushed her to within a centimetre of oblivion.

"Just stop!" Tomasz cried.

Peter nodded. "Then throw Balfus's trinket over the side."

Tomasz didn't hesitate. He dropped the amulet.

"Now pull her back. *Please!*"

"You understand at last," the creature chuckled. "Your greatest fear isn't storybook beasts and mythical monsters. It's that she will die and leave you, just like your father and grandpa did..." A smile creased that inhuman face. "Say hello to fear, Tomasz Kaczmarek!"

The smallest of shoves...

...and Tomasz's mother toppled into darkness.

"NO!"

Tomasz darted across the carriage, fell flat onto his stomach and snagged the hood of his mother's coat. Mercifully, the fabric held. With spears of agony lancing into his shoulder, Tomasz heard the cruel *pop* as his straining arm dislocated. Then, through aching fingers, he felt the pressure slacken as his mother scrambled onto the spoke below.

"She's okay," Tomasz panted. "She's okay."

And with those words his fear vanished. Twisting onto his back, he saw Peter leering over him, that cavernous mouth ready to feed.

"Too late," Tomasz grunted. "I'm not scared anymore."

With his good hand, he grasped the creature's robe and hauled himself upright.

The time had come. For the safety of the city a sacrifice must be made.

Tomasz whispered, "Now we'll see if an immortal's afraid of dying..."

Too late, the monster understood what was about to happen. Its talons slashed at Tomasz's face, but by then the pain didn't matter. He had already pulled Peter to the open door and now they were tipping chaotically into the sky. Locked together, the fearsome monster and the fearless boy plummeted through the cold October air while the ground rushed up to greet them...

*   *   *

The metal wall ratcheted upwards
and Balfus grabbed Tomasz by
the collar and drew him back into
the corridors of the horror house.
Tomasz stumbled in Balfus' wake
until they neared the entrance,
where he swatted the showman's
hand away.

"What the hell just happened?"

Balfus grinned and tapped his
uninjured neck. "Quite a show
you put on in there. I was

watching through a hatch, saw the whole thing. I've seen Peter draw out a million fears but I've never seen someone draw out *his*."

"I don't understand," Tomasz exclaimed. "Was any of that real?"

"Peter's real enough, and everything you learned about him is true. But the generator breaking down, his rampage through the fair, your mother and the Ferris wheel? Illusions conjured by my brother. But here's the thing: somehow you managed to show Peter *his* fears. The death of an immortal..." He gave Tomasz an appraising glance. "You're a strong-willed kid and no mistake."

"Right." Tomasz's smile was dazed. "Guess I get it from my grandpa."

Balfus slapped him on the shoulder. "We all live with fear, young man, but it's how we master that fear that makes us what we are. Ready to face the world again?"

"I think so." Tomasz nodded. "Yeah."

Outside, the fairground roared on as if nothing had happened — which of course it hadn't.

Balfus was making for the ticket booth when Tomasz called after him.

"What about Peter? Could he ever really get out?"

The showman sniffed. "If he does, I'll give you a call. In the meantime, perhaps you'll keep the Grimaldi secret to yourself?"

Tomasz nodded. At the bottom of the steps, he found Dugs waiting.

"What are you smiling at?" the bully growled.

Stopping dead, Tomasz treated Dugs to a look which sent him scuttling backwards. As he advanced on his tormentor, Tomasz could see the questions written on the bully's awestruck face: what is this strange new darkness dancing in Tomasz Kaczmarek's eyes? This sudden and scary confidence? This bright fearlessness, shining like a newborn star and cold as the cosmos?

"Hey, Dugs..." Tomasz rested his hand on the bully's shoulder and pulled him down so that he could whisper in his ear. "I think you've just wet yourself."

Also in the **RIVETS** series

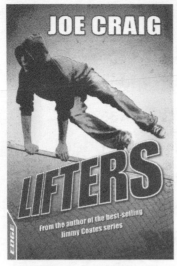

978 1 4451 0555 0 pb
978 1 4451 0850 6 eBook

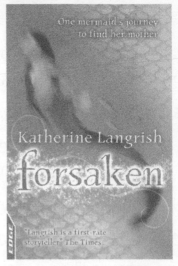

978 1 4451 0557 4 pb
978 1 4451 1073 8 eBook

978 1 4451 0556 7 pb
978 1 4451 0849 0 eBook

978 1 4451 0707 3 pb
978 1 4451 1072 1 eBook